TOMMY CAN'T STOP!

This book is dedicated to Tom Schumacher
—T.F.

For Liam, who never stays still!
—M.F.

Text copyright © 2015 by Tim Federle
Illustrations copyright © 2015 by Mark Fearing

All rights reserved. Published by Disney • Hyperion, an imprint of Disney Book Group. No part of this book may be reproduced or transmitted in any form or by any means, electronic or mechanical, including photocopying, recording, or by any information storage and retrieval system, without written permission from the publisher. For information address Disney • Hyperion, 125 West End Avenue, New York, New York 10023.

First Edition, April 2015
10 9 8 7 6 5 4 3 2 1
H106-9333-5-14349

Printed in Malaysia

Library of Congress Cataloging-in-Publication Data

Federle, Tim.
   Tommy can't stop! / by Tim Federle ; pictures by Mark Fearing. — First edition.
      pages cm
   Summary: Tommy has worn out his parents and sister with his bouncing, clomping, and leaping but when they convince him to try tap dancing, he finds it the perfect outlet for his energy.
   ISBN 978-1-4231-6917-8 — ISBN 1-4231-6917-4
   [1. Tap dancing—Fiction. 2. Family life—Fiction.] I. Fearing, Mark, illustrator. II. Title. III. Title: Tommy cannot stop.
   PZ7.F314Tom 2015
   [E]—dc23   2014015781

Reinforced binding
Visit www.DisneyBooks.com

TOMMY CAN'T STOP!

by Tim Federle

Pictures by Mark Fearing

Los Angeles   New York

Tommy's gotta bop.
(He can't keep still.)

"I'm a pogo stick!"
he boasts when he bounces.

"I'm a bulldozer!" he clamors when he kicks.

Tommy's gotta pop. (He can't keep quiet.)

"I'm an elephant!"
he calls when he clomps.

"I'm an antelope!"
he hollers when he hurdles.

("He's an *animal*," his sister pouts to their parents.)

Tommy's gotta stop. (His family can't keep up.)

"I'm *over* the elephant!"
his dad cries when he cleans.

"I'm tired of the
antelope!" his mom
trumpets before time-out.

("He belongs in a *zoo*," his sister bawls to her bestie.)

Everyone takes a turn tiring Tommy out.

Dad says: "Softball?"
But pogo sticks bounce off base.

Mom says: "Swim club!"
But bulldozers don't work underwater.

His sister says: "Tap class?
It's worth a *try*, Tommy...."

"I'm not putting on pink!"
he moans in the minivan.

"I'm not touching a tutu!"
he pleads in the parking lot.

("He's a doubting Thomas,"
his mom announces when they arrive.)

The tap teacher
begins bouncing.
(Wait! She twirls
like . . . *Tommy*!)

"You're a . . . pogo stick!"
he whispers as he watches.

"I call this a HOP."

(Everyone hops, but Tommy hops highest.)

The tap teacher kicks. (Now Tommy starts to smile.)
"You're a bulldozer!" he stammers as he stares.

"I call this a BRUSH!"

(Everyone brushes, but Tommy brushes boldest.)

The tap teacher clomps. (And Tommy's grin grows.)
"You're an elephant!" he bellows as he boogies.

"I call this a STAMP—
and don't call me an elephant!"

(Everyone stamps, but Tommy stamps strongest.)

The tap teacher hurdles. (Tommy giggles with glee.)
"You're an antelope!" he declares as he dances.

"I call it a LEAP!"

(Everyone leaps . . .

. . . but Tommy leaps

l – o – n –

g—e—s—t!)

TOMMY'S GOT TALENT!
(You can't stop a star.)

He beams when he bows . . .

. . . and glows when they gush.

And he'll never have to tiptoe to be Tommy!